Unofficial ROBLOX Book

THE GREAT JAILBREAK

NUBNEB

NubNeb

Make sure to check out my YouTube channel called NubNeb! I post hilarious family-friendly Roblox videos!

www.YouTube.com/NubNeb

ISBN-13: 978-1-947997-01-1

Chapter 1

Once upon a time, there was a miniature clump of ones and zeros, just floating peacefully in a sea of code. Life was great for the little clump, no chores, no school, just chilling in a void of blue while the world lived on without it.

Suddenly that all started to change when little by little the small clump started drifting away as if it got caught in an ocean current. It started slow, but soon it picked up some serious speed!

"Huh? Yo, what's happening?" asked the now growing clump numbers.

As the speed increased, more ones and zeros started adding to the clump, then whole lines of code started coming!

"WHAT IS HAPPENING TO ME!!!???" he screamed as his whole world started to change.

Without warning the clump of ones, zeros, and now whole scripts started combining together and morphing into solid parts! First, a head popped into existence, then a torso, and then two arms and two legs!

"WHAAAAAAAAAAAAAAAAAA!" he wailed as he got hurled around the void, almost as if he was on an invisible roller coaster.

ZWOOP

All of a sudden everything went silent and there was solid ground under his brand new feet.

"HEEEEELLLLPPPP MEEEEEEE!" he cried with his eyes jammed shut.

As he slowly opened his eyes, he saw a big group of people, some with morphs, and some without. Some with hair, hats, masks, and even wings, but they all had two things in common: All of them were wearing orange jumpsuits, and they were all staring at him.

"Where am I?" he asked. "Who am I!? Who are y'all?"

"You're in a prison, noob," someone replied with a scowl.

"I'm a noob? What's a noob?" he asked.

"Nah, fam. Don't listen to him, you're a nub," another one responded.

"Like, am I 'A Nub', or am I just 'Nub'?" the once clump of numbers questioned with actual confusion.

"Oh gosh..." the whole group moaned. Then someone face-palmed so hard their head popped off and started rolling away.

"I think I'm just going to stick with Nub if that's okay with y'all," Nub replied with a grin. "It's easier to introduce myself that way."

Before any more of the group could hurt themselves with more face-palms, something caught their attention right behind Nub. A few of them smirked, and the others grimaced.

"Look behind you, Nub!" a female voice squeaked from the crowd.

Nub turned his head to look behind. Standing behind him was another person, but he wasn't wearing orange. Instead, he was wearing a long sleeve, blue shirt, with two front pockets and a smudged, crooked, silver badge. Along with that, he wore blue canvas pants with an empty taser holster on the waist and a key card on the other side. His skin was as pale as the moon, and on his head were locks of hair that looked like two dozen bacon slices were just slapped on. The most worrying part about the bacon head was the fact that he had a taser in his hands, and it was pointed straight at Nub.

"Oh, hey there! I'm Nub, it's nice to-"

Before Nub could finish his introduction, two taser barbs plunged straight into his new pair of bum cheeks!

"AAAAHHHHHH" Nub screamed between each set of electric jolts. "WHAT" **ZAP** "DID" **ZAP** "I" **ZAP** "DO" **ZAP** "WRONG!?" **ZAAAP**

With a cloud of smoke, the tasing ended. Bacon Head looked down at the smoking body of Nub, gave a soulless smile, and walked straight back as if nothing happened.

"Uggghh," Nub moaned as picked himself up off the floor and turned to the crowd. "What just happened...?"

"Welcome to Jailbreak, Taser Tush," smirked a man with jet-black hair.

Chapter 2

As Nub plucked out the first taser barb, the crowd started going their own ways; all except for one.

"What do you want?" Nub asked, expecting another mean comment.

"I was just wondering if you're okay, but if you want me to go, that's perfectly fine with me," replied a brown haired girl.

"No, I'm sorry. I'm just not having the best day. I'm Nub, in case you missed it," Nub said with disappointment.

"Nice to meet you, Nub. My name's Emma. I'm guessing it's your first day logged in?"

"Yeah, I guess so. So what really is this place?" Nub asked.

"Well, as the black haired dude said-whose name is Cole, by the way, we're stuck in Jailbreak. From what I've heard, it's just one of the many worlds in the Server Nexus. But who am I to know. I logged in here 20 days ago and there hasn't been an escape since!"

As Nub got the second taser barb out, the prison bell rang three times, signaling that it was time for dinner.

"So, what's up with the guy who tased me?" Nub asked while they were waiting in the cafeteria line.

"Oh, him? Nobody knows really what's wrong with him. He probably has a clinker in his thinker. Legend has

it, if he catches you tr,
he'll tase you until your pa..
zling more than his bacon-like
would if you dropped it in a fryin,
pan!" Emma laughed.

Once they got their meal, they sat down to enjoy the brussel sprout and asparagus pudding with a side of broccoli purée, as best as they could.

Later that night, the jail bell rang alerting the guards to escort all of the prisoners to their cells, to get as much sleep as they could on the stone slab beds.

RiiiNNNG

"RISE AND SHINE, YA SMELLY TURDS! BREAKFAST IS GETTIN' COLD!" yelled a guard as he pressed a button that opened all of the gates.

Nub quickly got up and out of his cell and met up with Emma, who was in the middle of the crowd headed for breakfast.

"Morning, Nub!" Emma said cheerfully, "Did you get some sleep?" she asked.

"Once I got comfortable," Nub replied with a smile.

Out of the corner of his eye, Nub saw Cole approaching.

"Hey! Look who it is. Morning, Taser Tush!" Cole taunted.

"Leave him alone, Cole. He's new," Emma responded.

"It's alright, Emma. I'm not scared of him," Nub responded, attempting to ignore Cole.

"Yeah, Emma. Let the little stinker defend himself!" Cole sneered.

"Wait, WHAT DID YOU CALL ME!?" Nub raised his voice in shock.

"A stinker, you stinker!" Cole retorted, begging for a fight.

"Hey!? I don't stink!" Nub replied defensively as he lifted his arm to smell under his pits.

"Oh yeah? When was the last time you took a shower?" Cole asked with a grin.

"I took one- well..." Nub tried looking back into his past, but he remembered he first logged in just yesterday. "Wait, that's not fair!" Nub complained.

"Exactly, ya stinker," Cole laughed with a grin, "And if you don't like it, we can finish this out in the courtyard after lunch, where there is more room to be... aggressive!" Cole snarled.

Emma gave Nub a look of warning.

"I'll be there!" Nub answered with a nod.

Cole went his own way, and Nub and Emma grabbed some breakfast and sat down.

"Nub, you better not go out there," Emma warned, before taking a bite of green oatmeal.

"What? To fight? It's too late now, I already agreed. If I back out now, I'll be called a chicken!" Nub responded

"So what!? That would be better than whatever the guards might do to you if they catch you fighting!" Emma said, "Don't take the bait, Nub. Fighting never helps anything."

"Don't worry, I got this" Nub assured.

After breakfast, Nub went back to his cell and started throwing some practice punches.

"Ugh, I can't believe he called me a stinker... He's the real stinker!" Nub vented between punches. "Hello Cole, I'm about to beat your blocky bum!" Nub said, practicing his entrance speech, "Nah, what about: 'I'm going to knock the blocks out of you!' No, too aggressive. 'Kind sir, may you please withdraw the title of 'stinker' from my name please?'" Nub laughed. "I'll just go in arms flinging, and punches flying!" Nub said with a confident smirk.

As the lunch bell rang, Nub caught up with Emma to choke down some food and feed all the butterflies in his stomach.

"Even though I know that there is nothing I can do to change your mind, I might as well ask if you even have a plan," Emma said with disapproval.

"Of course! I'm going to walk up, slam him with a right hook to the face, then give him an uppercut straight to the jaw, free of charge!" Nub said with an excited grin.

"That's funny," Emma laughed, "But for real, you did plan something out, right?"

"Wait, what do you mean? That is my plan!"

"Nub! It's not that type of fight! It's a-"

RiiiNNNG

The jail bell, signaling it was courtyard time, interrupted Emma right before she could finish her sentence.

"Lunch is over. Wish me luck!" Nub said, totally disregarding everything that Emma said.

"I got this! I got this! I got this!" Nub pumped himself up as he walked to the courtyard.

As he got closer and closer to his destination, he started hearing what sounded like a big group of people cheering.

"Uh, I didn't know he was bringing an audience!" Nub thought to himself, as sweat started rolling down his forehead. He got to the entrance of the courtyard and saw a crowd of about 20 people, all making a big ring. In the middle of the ring was a man holding a spoon, yelling random things at the crowd. At the back of the ring, but still inside, Cole stood tall with a black hoodie over his head, and a huge, gold, necklace hanging around his neck. Before Nub could go right back to his cell and contemplate his life decisions, the man with a spoon saw him.

"Hey, there he is! Come on down Nub, and give us your rapper name!" the man yelled into his spoon as if it was a microphone.

"Wait, what?" asked Nub as he stumbled his way to the crowd.

"Alllllright!" the announcer yelled. "DJ WaitWut is in the house!"

"DJ? I thought this was a fist fight!?" Nub said as he pushed himself inside the ring.

"What? A fist fight? Were you raised in a prison? We're more civilized than that!" the announcer scoffed.

"Well, technically-" Nub started

"Nah! This is a RAP BATTLE!!!" he interrupted.

Once the man said that, the crowd blew up with cheers!

"WHO'S READY FOR SOME FIRE!?" he yelled, "We have DJ WaitWut versus Mr. [Content Deleted]!"

The crowd started cheering again, obviously biased toward Cole.

"Mr [Content Deleted], start us off!" The announcer finished as he walked to the side of the ring, to make room for Cole.

"Yo yo!" Cole started.

"[Content Deleted] in dah house!

"Time to crush this punk like a little baby mouse!"

The crowd oohed.

"Challenging me? You must be a dupe,

"I'ma step on you like stinky dog p##p!

"What? You couldn't read that?

"Oh yeah, forgot you're still stuck in safe chat!" Cole continued.

"OOOOOH!" the crowd yelled, starting to get unruly.

"You came into my prison,

"Without my own permission,

"I have a strong suspicion,

"That you have a mental condition."

By now the crowd was roaring with laughter.

"Your body is so blocky, you need a physician.

"Nah, forget that, fam. You need a magician!

"It doesn't take a statistician,

"To know that you're dumber than an American politician.

"Your lack of bathing gives you a bad emission,

"A smell so shocking you need an electrician!

"The smell's so piercing it wrecks the competition,

"Ten times stronger than any ammunition," Cole finished as he plugged his nose and fell to the ground.

The announcer had to use every last bit of his energy shouting into his spoon to try to keep the crowd from bursting out the roof.

"Now that is spitting bars from behind bars!" The announcer said to the crowd while clapping his hands together. "Alright DJ WaitWut, time to show us what you got!" he pointed to Nub as a few of the crowd members picked themselves off the ground.

"Yo... What's up y'all!" Nub started.

"Not your chances of winning!" Someone piped up from the crowd, while others oohed.

"Yeah, I agree," Nub mumbled quietly as he cleared his throat.

"Yo, I live in a hut... I have a big butt!" Nub spit out, without thinking. "My body is stocky, I like teriyaki."

By now everyone was cracking up.

"You got this, Nub!" Emma's voice rang out from the crowd.

"Yeah. I got this," Nub whispered with fake confidence.

"Yo, you callin me stinker,

"But at least I am a thinker,

"When I drive I use my blinker,

"I'ma wreck your little finger,

"Hook, line, and sinker," Nub blurted out.

Though it didn't make much sense, apparently it rhymed enough to get everyone's attention!

"I really should let it go,

"But hmm, how about NO.

"Now that I am in the flow,

"I'ma squash you like guano!"

The crowd started cheering now that there was a chance for a good battle.

"Your gold chain is so cheap,

"It's from a gas station.

"If your eyebrows were a city

"They'd lack in population,

"I have a fascination

"With your hairlines declination,

"But you have acceleration

"In your nose hair generation!"

By now the crowd was roaring with laughter, just as much as they did with Cole's.

"This is a proclamation,

"A sort of condemnation,

"To end your perpetration,
"Of verbal mutilation.

"Your only limitation
"Is your lack in vindication,
"No parental validation
"Which leads to aberration!

"This wasn't a roast,
"It was a cremation!" Nub finished
with a smirk.

By now most of the crowd was
jumping up and down, screaming inaudible things out of excitement, or lying
on the ground, spasming, because they
just couldn't handle the heat.

"Holy crab cakes!" yelled the announcer. "Now THAT is spitting fire!"
He finished with his eyes as big as tomatoes.

"Thanks!" Nub laughed, wondering where all that came from.

Suddenly the whole crowd went silent, and tensed up. Nub, with all of the adrenaline pumping through him, didn't notice it.

"The fire was so hot, I bet it would've fried that stupid Bacon Head's hair!" Nub laughed.

There was no response from the crowd.

"He's right behind me, isn't he?" Nub asked with a scowl.

ZAAAP

Chapter 3

"Ugghh" Nub moaned.

His head and his butt hurt. He slowly opened his eyes and saw that he was laying on his cell's stone slab bed. Just then Emma walked by and looked in.

"Finally you're awake! Took you long enough, sleeping beauty!" Emma said with a laugh.

"Was I out for long? What happened?" Nub asked, rubbing his head.

"Well... about a month I believe?" Emma questioned herself.

"A MONTH!?!?" Nub shouted with surprise.

Emma laughed. "Just kidding, it was only a day, but it felt like a month!"

"Oh good, and why's that?"

"Well, no one knows why, but ever since the rap battle, all of the guards have really tightened security! They have decreased meal time, and they have almost taken away free time completely!" Emma answered with disgust. "They're are probably preparing for a jailbreak, and I think that you and I should give it to them!" Emma said.

"You mean escape? Won't they kill us if they catch us?" Nub asked, surprised by Emma's change of mind.

"Well, they'd have to catch us first!" Emma responded with a smirk.

Nub chuckled and shook his head.

"Just think of all the other worlds just waiting to be explored!" Emma dreamed.

"So how are you planning on getting us out of here?"

"Alright," Emma started, excited to share her master plan.

"Step one: we make sure we are close to a guard, so he can hear us, and then we start discussing how we found a tunnel in the courtyard."

"Step two: after dinner we separate from the crowd and find some place to hide."

"Step three: once the guards see that we are not in our cells after dinner, they'll start looking for us. Hopefully, that one guard will tell them about the 'tunnel' in the courtyard, and they will all go there!"

"Step four: we jump into an air vent, crawl to the security control room, and figure out how to escape from there!" Emma finished explaining.

"Dang, you get a lot done when I'm knocked out!" Nub answered jokingly.

"That's what happens when you take away my free time!" Emma said, glaring at a guard through the doorway. "So are you in or out?" She asked.

"Pfft, I'm totally in! When do we start?" Nub asked excitedly.

"Is tonight too soon?" Emma asked with a smirk.

The day slowly passed on until the dinner bell finally rang.

RiiiNNNG

"YOUR FIVE MINUTE DINNER BREAK STARTS NOW, YA TOILET FLOATERS!" a guard shouted, as a horde of prisoners stampeded to the cafeteria.

Once Nub and Emma got their food, they sat down at the table nearest to a guard.

"Yo, Nub," Emma started, whispering loud enough for the guard to hear. "I heard there's a secret tunnel in the courtyard!"

The guard looked over at their table, then looked back as he pretended he couldn't hear them continue the conversation.

A few short minutes later, the main guard started yelling again. "TIME IS UP, YA FAT PIGS! LAST ONE TO THEIR CELL GETS TO BE TARGET PRACTICE FOR THE NEW RECRUITS!" Before he even finished the threat, a stampede of people started pushing each other over, jumping over tables, and sprinting to their cells. Nub and Emma used this opportunity to sneak into the janitor's closet.

"Did anyone see us?" Emma whispered.

"Nah, I think we're good," Nub whispered back.

They heard some racket outside the door.

"NO PLEASE! I'm sorry, I tripped!" Someone squeaked.

"Not my problem," Another person's voice boomed. "You're the last one to your cell."

ZAAAP

"They weren't messing around." Nub whispered, his eyes wide open.

Emma nodded no.

They waited in the janitor's closet until they heard some more commotion.

"Sir! We are missing three inmates!" a voice said.

"WHAT!?" another voice shouted.

"I think they said something about a tunnel in the courtyard!" the first voice squeaked.

"ALL GUARDS TO THE COURTYARD, NOW!" shouted the second voice into a radio. "The boss is going to kill me."

"Who's the other one?" Nub whispered.

"I don't know, but as long as they don't get in our way, I don't care," Emma replied.

Once they heard all the guards stomp to the courtyard they opened the closet door and peeked out.

"I think it's clear!" Nub whispered looking through the cracked door.

"Alright, follow me!" Emma ordered.

She led him out of the room, down the hallway, and to an air vent on the side of the wall.

"Please don't be locked," She whispered to herself as she pulled on the air vent.

CHERRNK

The air vent whined as it opened regretfully.

"Yes!" Emma said with celebration.

"Ladies first!" Nub replied jokingly motioning her to climb in.

"My pleasure, I'd rather not stare at your butt the whole time we're crawling in there," Emma retorted as she climbed in, with Nub in tail.

"AWWWWCHUUU" Nub sneezed. "It's dusty in here."

"Yeah, let's hope the AC doesn't turn on," Emma prayed.

As soon as she said it they heard a deep humming start.

"Great job, you jinxed it," Nub said hopelessly, preparing for the mother of all sneeze attacks.

Right then, they were hit with a blast of cold air, which stirred up every particle of dust.

"GO, GO, GO!" Emma yelled above the sound of whooshing air, her mouth filling up with dust and hair.

Nub took a deep breath, making his cheeks as big as a pufferfish, and crawled after her.

They crawled down the aluminum tunnel until they saw another air vent grill and looked through it.

"Nope, that's the cafeteria," Emma examined through the grill. The AC finally flipped back off. "Time to keep crawling," she said as her knees were clanging in the metal shaft.

They continued crawling through the ventilation tunnel until they found another vent.

"OH GOSH!" Emma exclaimed as she slapped her hands over her eyes.

"What is it?" Nub asked as he crawled his way over to see. "It's the Men's Bathroom," he laughed before they continued on.

They crawled for what felt like 15 minutes and started to hear a bunch of ruckus.

"We are getting closer to the cell block," Nub whispered as they continued crawling.

"Yep! I think this one's the one!" Emma said once they made it to another grill. "No guards. Our freedom is just sitting here for us!"

"Then what are we waiting for? We hop in there, press a button that opens up some doors, climb back through and get outta here!" Nub said excitedly, already tasting freedom! Unless of course, that was what dust tasted like.

They popped the grill open and after one final check they hopped in.

"Uuuuuuuhh" Emma groaned with her jaw on the floor.

There was a wall covered in security camera monitors from all over the prison. They could see all the prisoners in the cell block and all the guards tearing up the courtyard. On the other side of the room there was a long hallway and at the end of it was a wall of buttons. To their horror, the hallway was

full of laser traps, platforms f
lava, and a giant spinner, sitting over
green, bubbling, acid.

"Well, Nub, I'll guard the door,"
Emma said laughing nervously after
taking a big gulp.

"You didn't tell me about this!" Nub
said, sweat rolling down his pale forehead.

"I didn't even know about this!" Emma responded, low-key freaking out.
"Now I hate to rush you, but they can
only wreck the courtyard up for so
long!"

"We could've at least done Rock-
Paper-Scissors," Nub mumbled as he
walked to the first obstacle.

The first series of obstacles were a
bunch spy movie-like lasers, as if he
was in a bank. The first laser was at
knee height, from one side of the wall
to the other.

"Easy," Nub commentated to himself as he stepped over it.

The next set of lasers were at the same knee height but another laser was going diagonally from the ceiling to the floor.

"Still easy," he said to himself as ducked, and stepped over.

The farther he went, the more lasers were added. Soon he got to one where there were two diagonal lasers making a cross at the center, plus the laser at knee height, and one more going sideways across his chest.

"I take it back, it's not easy any-more," Nub moaned as he started to crawl through.

"Watch out, Nub!" Emma screamed making him freeze.

His foot was just fractions of an inch away from a laser. He carefully corrected himself then continued through.

"Nailed it!" Nub said excitedly as he shot his hands into the air in celebration.

"NUB!" Emma screamed as her eyes got really wide.

Nub looked up at his arm and saw that his hand was blocking one of the lasers.

"ONE LIFE DOWN," a robotic voice exclaimed through a speaker on the wall. "ONE LIFE LEFT."

"Sorry," Nub whispered as Emma took a sigh of relief.

Nub continued through the sets of lasers and he finally made it to the last one. To make it past, he would have to go through a really skinny, diagonal opening. If he was even an inch off in any direction, he would touch a laser and bring all the cops to the security room.

"Here goes nothing!" Nub whispered to himself as he sucked in every bit of his blocky gut.

He positioned himself up with the opening, stuck one leg through, then brought the first half of his body through.

"Almost..." Nub moaned as he held his breath.

Nub lifted his other leg up and put it through, then he guided the rest of his body past the diagonal slot.

"Like a glove!" Nub exclaimed.

"Now I only have to make it over this these lava platforms, and past the acid spinner and I'm good!" Nub thought to himself, hopelessly.

The next challenge was a big pool of bubbling lava, with a few floating bricks that he would have to jump onto to get across.

"How'd they even get lava in here?" Nub asked himself as he planned his next steps. It was a long, rectangular pool, with three floating bricks that went from big to small.

"I guess I'll just jump onto the first one, and play it from there!" Nub thought to himself. With a few feet for a running start, he leaped over the gurgling lava, towards the first platform.

"Whoa!" Nub exclaimed as he planted his feet, with only a few inches to spare on the platform. He rocked back and forth as if he was on a small raft surfing over ocean waves.

Now he had two more platforms to jump onto before he made it past the steaming lava. The middle platform was just in legs reach of Nub.

"So if I just reach my leg over and step onto it, I wouldn't have to jump to it and risk falling off!" Nub thought to himself.

He picked up his right leg, stretched it across the lava, and planted it onto the second platform.

"Easy as pie!" Nub thought, excited to be halfway done with the lava pit.

Right before he was going to bring his other leg over, the two platforms starting floating in separate directions, forcing him to do a split!

"AHHHH! Help Emma!" Nub pan-icked.

"Pull yourself together, Nub!" Emma screamed from across the hallway.

"A little easier said than done!" Nub yelled back. His legs were stretched all the way apart, and his waist was only a few studs over the lava. Any professional gymnast would've been proud.

"I don't wanna become barbecue!" Nub wailed, as his feet started slipping from the platform.

"Nub!" Emma screamed in terror as her new best friend slipped butt first into the pit of boiling hot lava.

"WHAAAAAA!" Nub wailed, with his eyes jammed shut, expecting to be engulfed in flames.

THUD

"Ow..." Nub whimpered. He opened his eyes and found he was just resting on the lava as if it was a solid brick.

"HAH!" Nub laughed in celebration. "I'M ALIVE!"

"it's just a screen!" Emma joined in.

"I knew it was-"

"*BOOP, out of lives. Commence lockdown!*" the robotic voice announced.

Before Nub and Emma could react, both the doors and the air vents locked shut, and prison alarms started blaring.

"Nub! They're coming!" Emma shouted as she looked at the security monitors.

Without responding, Nub picked himself off of the virtual lava and started sprinting back to Emma, running straight through the lasers.

"The vents are locked from this side!" Emma panicked.

"We gotta get out of here!" Nub replied, pounding on the door, desperate to save his tush from another round of electrocution.

"They're getting closer!" Emma warned, checking the cameras again.

Just then they heard the sound of footsteps coming towards them.

Nub positioned himself in front of the door, looked out the small rectangular window, and prepared for his, and his bum's impending doom.

Suddenly the footsteps stopped.

Nub took a big gulp and a deep breath.

"SUP LADIES!" Cole's face leaped into the window frame, jump scaring Nub and Emma.

"AHH!" Nub screamed as he stumbled back. "What are you doing here? Never mind, just open the door and let us out!" Nub yelled through the door.

"And why should I do that?" Cole responded with a smirk.

"Because I said so!" Nub replied, running low on patience.

"Geez, you're a demanding one, aren't you," Cole noted with sarcasm.

"BOYS! They will be here any minute!" Emma interrupted their conversation with panic.

"Alright, alright. What's the password?" Cole instigated.

"Cole, I will murder you if you don't open up this door," Nub threatened, on his last string.

Cole yawned and checked his invisible watch.

Nub glared at Cole but kept his mouth shut.

"Nub! Just say it!" Emma said, equally annoyed.

After a few seconds of glaring, Nub finally got over his pride.

"FINE!" Nub said defeated. "Pleeeeeeeease."

"There we go, little Nub Nub! Let's go," Cole said, smiling with his victory, before opening the door from the outside.

Nub clenched his fist, then he and Emma started following Cole through the winding prison hallways towards the cell block.

Chapter 4

"So what are you doing out?" Emma asked, breaking the silence as their feet pounded on the concrete floor.

"Well..." Cole started with a huff. "I WAS going to escape through the gate in the courtyard, but SOMEONE brought all the cops over there!" He said, glaring at Emma and Nub. "I was just about to take the front panel off of the electric box, in hopes of hot wiring it, but then every cop and their brother came rushing in. Luckily, I'm such a pro, that I made it out of there without being seen," he finished with a smirk.

"Sorry about that," Nub laughed sarcastically.

Suddenly they started hearing a whole army of footsteps coming their way.

"Hurry, we gotta hide!" Emma said looking around the wide, empty hallway.

"There's a janitor's closet just down the next turn," Cole said as he started sprinting through the hallway and taking a left turn.

Nub and Emma quickly caught up and they all entered back into the same janitor's closet the night started with.

"Ugh, what is it with these closets tonight?" Nub whined, trying not to breathe in the air which smelled of cleaners and bug poison.

"Must be a sign about your poor personal hygiene," Cole chuckled.

"Shhh!" Emma hushed them before another argument broke out.

To ease his boredom of waiting for the search party to walk by, Nub started digging around the closet.

"You know, with how nasty this prison is I doubt they even use half of these cleaners," Nub joked.

"Yeah, they probably put more of it in our food in an attempt to make it taste better," Cole snorted.

Nub laughed and continued digging through the bottles. He grabbed a bottle of toilet cleaner, lifted it up and scooted it out of the way, behind it was a small, rolled up piece of paper.

"What is this?" Nub asked, puzzled, as he reached for the paper.

"What is what?" Cole asked back, not expecting much.

"It's like a small scroll," Nub replied, intrigued with the note.

"Probably a tutorial on how to clean the toilets correctly," Emma joked.

"Well then read it, I'm going to need it once I get out of here," Cole said with a laugh.

"Alright, here it goes," Nub said, unrolling the paper and clearing his throat.

Journal Entry #1337

Today I, xXSuperSniperXx, am going to escape this dreaded place. I have been locked in here for over 420 days, and not one person has been able to escape. I am here to change that, and if you find this message, I hope you can find freedom too.

I am going to share the key part of my plan, but in case you are one of the guards, I am going to put it in a riddle. The guards here lack a brain and won't be able to figure it out.

Smash the pot where relief is found,
Yes, the one where floaters abound.
Down in the river where your adventure comes from, the farther you swim, you'll be nearer to home

That's the end of the riddle, my friend. I wish you good luck, and maybe one day you will see me out in one of the other vast worlds!

"What kind of a name is 'xXSuperSniperXx'?" Cole scoffed.

"Who cares about his name!? We might have a way out of here!" Emma responded excitedly.

"Yeah! What do you think the riddle means though?" Nub asked.

"Probably have to smash some cooking pot in a pool, then go swimming in it?" Cole responded with a blank face.

"Oh shut up, Cole," Emma said, rolling her eyes.

"Alright, so the first part is 'Smash the pot where relief is found. Yes, the one where floaters abound' What are some pots where relief is found?" Nub asked.

"A toilet," Cole snorted joking.

"Cole," Emma glared.

"Wait a second," Nub started stroking his invisible beard. "I think Cole might be right!" He finished with sudden realization.

"Wait, what?" Cole replied with surprise.

"Yeah! Whenever you need to take a dump, where do you go?" Nub asked grinning.

"The toilet," Cole answered, giggling while Emma face palmed.

"And what happens when the toilet doesn't flush properly?" Nub asked, also giggling but trying not to be too loud and alert the search parties.

"The floaters come back!" Cole said, about to lose it.

"So we're just supposed to smash the toilets?" Emma asked with a grossed out face.

"I don't know for sure, but maybe the last part of the riddle will tell us!" Nub said. "Down in the river where your adventure comes from, the farther you swim, you'll be nearer to home," Nub restated.

"Well if your toilet theory is correct, the 'River' could very well be a sewage pipe," Emma said with a disgusted face.

Both Cole and Nub nodded in agreement.

"Where do you think 'Home' is?" Cole asked.

"Maybe some safe house the pipe leads to?" Emma offered.

"Possibly, but what are some 'Homes' that are in this jail?" Nub probed.

"The kitchen?" Cole asked.

"The jail cells?" Emma added.

"After 'Taco Tuesday', the bathroom," Cole snickered."

Emma groaned.

"What about Home Plate, in the courtyard?" Nub asked with curiosity.

Both Emma and Nub looked at Cole, him being the most experienced person in the Janitor's Closet.

Cole looked down at his feet, trying to recollect his thoughts, then it suddenly came to him. "Actually, way back when I first logged in to this world, the guards were actually chill enough to let us play kickball," Cole reminisced. "Some kid went up to kick the ball, completely missed it, and just sent the home base flying. It might've been me," Cole coughed out. "But anyway, there was some sort of hatch underneath. Before I could investigate it, a group of prisoners quickly covered it back up and looked around to make sure none of the guards saw it. " Cole continued. "I didn't understand it back then, but I guess that's where all of those guys escaped the next night," Cole finished with what seemed like anger in his eyes.

"Wow, well I guess that's our way out!" Nub said excitedly.

"Well, only half of it. That'll get us to the courtyard, but then we need to go from there," Emma responded.

"Well let's get out of this closet, sneak back into our cells and plan it tomorrow!" Cole said with a yawn.

The group checked to make sure there was no one near the closet, then made their way back to the cells without being seen.

Chapter 5

The breakfast bell rang, and the new group of friends made their way to the cafeteria.

"Do you think any of the guards know it was us that escaped?" Emma asked while waiting in line for the week-old scrambled eggs.

"No telling, but their security will definitely be high for a bit, so we better lay low," Cole answered, looking over his shoulder.

"Sounds good, though we still need to get together and come up with a plan," Nub said, anxious to get out.

"Yeah, maybe during free time we can work something up," Emma agreed.

The crew finished their breakfast, straightened up their cells, and waited for the bell to ring signifying free time.

RiiiNNNG

"About time," Nub noted impatiently.

All three of them walked separately to the courtyard, in hopes that they wouldn't raise suspicion. Once they made it there, Cole hopped on a treadmill, and Nub and Emma started lifting weights.

"So," Emma huffed between breaths, "are we going to help anyone else escape, or just ourselves?"

"I would say the more the merrier. It'll create more chaos and decrease our odds of being captured on our way out," Nub thought out loud.

"Yes, but that would make it harder to be stealthy," Emma responded.

"I think strategically it would be better with fewer people, But I know a lot of these guys and girls have been locked up for ages," Cole said, slowing down to a walk. "And when the group of prisoners who I first logged in with left me behind, I made a promise to myself: if I ever had a chance to escape, I'd share it and get as many people out of this awful prison as I could!" Cole finished passionately.

"Whoa, bro. Where's the cinematic music when you need it?" Nub said with wide eyes.

"Yeah, well I guess that's decided!" Emma said, equally surprised.

"So, any idea on on the full plan?" Cole asked, looking at Nub.

"Alright, so here's what I put together," Nub started. "Right after dinner, I'm going to get inside the air vent and make it to the security room, hopefully they won't notice just one person missing. Y'all will smash all the toilets in your cells, crawl to the courtyard, and Cole will rewire the courtyard gate and get you all out to the parking lot. From there, the only thing between us and freedom, is the front gate! And that's where I come in. I have to make it past all the lasers, lava, and acid, then get to the button which will open the main gate! From there it's every man for himself!" Nub finished smugly. "Or, every woman for herself, in your case Emma," he added.

"Did you get any sleep last night?" Cole laughed.

"Nah, not much," Nub chuckled back.

"Well, it sounds like a solid plan to me!" Emma said.

"So how are we going to let all of our other inmates know, without making the guards suspicious?" Nub asked.

"I say we do it the old fashion way," Cole smirked. "Pass a note around the cafeteria!"

Chapter 6

Tonight was the night. Either they'd escape, or they'd die trying!

Thankfully the note got passed around discreetly, and not one guard noticed. Once each prisoner read the note, they all did one thing in common: they only ate a couple bites of their food. It might've been because they were nervous, or they didn't want a mess in their toilet before they had to smash it.

"ALRIGHT, YOU UNGRATEFUL LOGS, BACK TO YOUR CELLS! IT'S

SLEEPY TIME!" the high ranking guard yelled.

The first part of the plan was working perfectly. The prisoners created such a big ruckus that no one saw Nub slip away, and go directly into the air vent. Some prisoners might've been going a little too crazy with the stampede back to their cells. They managed to flip a few tables, and knock over almost every chair!

As Nub started making his way through the air vent, Emma, Cole, and the rest of the prisoners made it to their cells.

"So are we actually getting out of here, tonight?" A prisoner named Jack whispered nervously to Emma from another cell.

"Yep! Once the guards leave the cell room, we'll either move or smash our toilets, and crawl through the sewage pipes, just like the note said!" Emma quietly replied, secretly praying the riddle was true.

The guards went through the cell block and did a lazy count.

"Alright, Arnold. I counted all 42," One guard said with his eyes half closed.

"Well, uh, I counted 41," the other guard replied.

"Oh shut up. You don't even know how to count, you blockhead," The first guard said before dragging Arnold out with him.

A few minutes after the guards left, Cole's voice rang through the room.

"Alright, ladies and gents! Who's ready to get out of this garbage dump!" he yelled.

The rest of the prisoners shouted in celebration.

"Alright, I like it!" Cole said with a smirk. "Well y'all read the note that we passed around, either move or smash your toilet, and hopefully there should be a sewage pipe big enough to crawl through!" He instructed.

A few people groaned, others laughed, but no one seemed very hopeful. Suddenly a big crash echoed across the room! The biggest prisoner of the group, named Tinsel, drop kicked his toilet and completely smashed it into dust.

"They were right!" Tinsel shouted excitedly before jumping into the pipe which was sloped down like a water slide.

"Hurray!" The whole cell block celebrated before beating up their own poor, innocent toilets.

Toilet seats were flying everywhere, and people started jumping down their drain pipe for the ride of their life!

"AHHHHHH!" Emma screamed as she plummeted down her drain. The only thing that made her close her mouth was the thought of what was in the sewer water that was spraying into her face.

The ride finally ended when the pipe led to a long rectangular tunnel filled with stagnant chest-deep water that smelled worse than the remains of Taco Tuesday. The walls were lined with all the ends of the individual cell's drain pipes, and at the far end of the tunnel was a ladder that hopefully led to whichever 'home' the riddle talked about.

"Ewww," Emma moaned, trying not to vomit as she waded through the surprise-filled liquid.

Sploosh! Splash! Splush! Splop!

Cole and three other inmates splashed into the tunnel.

"Nasty..." Cole muttered after taking a big whiff of the smell.

Once all the prisoners made to the ladder at the end of the hallway, Cole started climbing up.

"Time to find out where this tunnel leads!" Cole announced while tugging on a hatch door that was positioned over the ladder.

Keeeeerchunk

The hatch groaned as it opened slowly. Sure enough, the bottom side of the courtyards home plate was staring right down at them.

The crowd burst into cheers before Emma quickly shushed them so they didn't wake up any guards.

"Alright everybody," Cole announced, just loud enough for the crowd to hear. "So here's what's going to happen. I'm going to hotwire the courtyard gate to open up, and that will lead us to the parking lot. From there, Nub will open up the main gate and then we'll be free!" He finished as he lifted the home plate out of the way and crawled through.

By this time, Nub finally made it to the empty security room and dropped in.

"Here goes nothing," he said, as he positioned himself in front of the lasers.

This time he made it through without touching any of them. Now he just had to make it through the lava floaters and the acid spinner.

"I got it this time," Nub mumbled with fake confidence. If he failed, everyone would be put back in jail because of him. They might never be able to see any other worlds for the rest of their lives!

Nub leaped towards the first block. He thought his feet planted, but they didn't stick. He fell on his butt and one of his feet dangled off the edge, touched the holographic lava, and triggered the computer.

"One life left," the robotic voice squawked at him.

Back at the courtyard, the inmates were getting more and more nervous as the time ticked on.

"How's it going?" Emma asked Cole.

"Not good," he grumbled back. He has been working on this electric box for over 10 minutes. They're lucky a guard hasn't walked out and seen the whole group yet!

The cables were an absolute mess, and Cole was already extremely frustrated.

ZAP

A shock of electricity jolted into Cole's hand and through his body.

"AHHHH!" Cole screamed in frustration. "THIS STUPID CHUNK OF METAL!" he vented.

Cole pulled his hand back, then sent his fist soaring into the electric box in a fit of rage.

Baa doop

The gate opened with a cheerful chime.

"Nice job, buddy!" One of the prisoners patted him on the back while making his way to the gate.

"Yeah, that's one way to do it," Emma chuckled. "Now it's all up to Nub."

Nub resituated himself on the floating block and prepared to jump to the second, smaller block.

He leaped, his arms out like wings for balance, and landed on the second block successfully. He took a deep breath and observed the last block. It looked just like the others, only smaller.

"Here we go!" Nub said, pumping himself up.

He lowered his stance, then sprung towards the final platform. His aim was perfect, he was on track for a perfect landing!

bloop

The block disappeared from under his feet and he came crashing down into the holographic lava once again.

"WHAT!?" Nub shrieked. "That's not fair!"

The whole room was illuminated with flashing red lights, and ear piercing alarms started screaming.

"You know what?" Nub asked rebelliously. "If you're not playing fair, then neither am I!"

He picked himself off the ground and started sprinting towards the control console. Once he got to the spinner which was suspended over the green, slimy acid, he just ducked underneath the spinner, and then continued running. Turns out the acid was just a hologram too.

"TAKE THIS!" Nub screamed as he started pressing every button he saw.

"Oh no," Emma said quietly as she turned her head to Cole. They heard the prison alarms blaring which meant Nub must be in trouble.

Before any of them could think about going back and helping Nub, chaos started to break out.

The main gate jolted open, police garages opened up, the cars all turned on by themselves, every single door in the prison opened on its own, and all the spotlights used for escapees were flinging around like it was a disco party!

"Alright, everyone, hop inside any vehicle you can find and let's get out of here!" Cole ordered.

"I hope that did something!" Nub said before turning around and sprinting toward the now opened door; not even worrying about crawling back through the air vent.

He took a right when he got out of the door and kept his eyes straight ahead as his feet started slamming on the prison floor.

He was running so fast everything was a blur. He took another right, then a left, then another right. Suddenly he started hearing shouts from behind him.

"We got one on the run!" a guard's voice rang out, followed by the pounding of footsteps.

The farther Nub ran, the closer the footsteps got. Nub took a left turn into a hallway which led to the courtyard. There were only seconds left before the guard caught up. Just as Nub made it to the door, a helicopter appeared right outside, allowing him to barrel into it.

"AHHH!" Nub shouted, as he crashed into the seats. In a split second, the helicopter jolted back into the air before the guards could make it in.

"Yo! Who's flying this thing?" Nub asked, hoping it wasn't a guard.

"How ya doing buddy?" Cole's voice rang out through the helicopter intercom.

"Nice ride," Nub chuckled.

He looked out the opening and saw quite a scene. A few prisoners were in helicopters flying out of the prison, and others were in sporty police cars, squealing their tires as they sped from the prison towards their first taste of freedom.

Then out of the police quarters swarmed what seemed like hundreds of guards running to their vehicles. The remaining helicopters took off, but this time they had police lights flashing, signifying that they weren't there to play.

"So where's Emma?" Nub asked Cole as they started to fly towards a city.

"She should be okay. She hopped in a police car with a few other inmates," Cole responded. "But, it looks like a few escapees might encounter some trouble soon," he said with worry.

Twenty police cars raced out of the prison with their sirens on, in hot pursuit of the escapees. They quickly caught up and started pushing the criminal's cars to spin them out of control.

"Oh no," Nub said grimacing.

Just then a police helicopter rammed into a criminal helicopter and knocked it out of the sky.

"Should we go help them?" Nub asked Cole, feeling helpless.

"I wish we could, but they are loaded with weapons and tasers. It would really just be suicide," Cole answered, equally disheartened.

As they got farther and farther away from the prison, Nub could see more and more prisoners being taken down and arrested. He just hoped Emma was not one of them.

Chapter 7

A knock on the safe house door startled Nub awake.

"Emma?" he asked with hope. So far, she had not been seen. Only 10 of the 42 prisoners had made it to the designated safe house, and that included him and Cole.

He made his way to the door and slowly opened it, making sure it wasn't a guard.

Nub's heart dropped when he saw it wasn't his friend, but he was still glad to see that it was another prisoner, whose name was Luke.

"Nub! We gotta save them! They're going to die!" Luke said frantically. His face and arms were covered in scratches and bruises.

"Whoa, slow down Luke! Tell us what happened," Nub said while ushering Luke into the house, and waking up the others.

Once Luke got situated, he started telling his story.

"Well as you probably know, once we got in the cars and began our escape, the guards started chasing us. They weren't taking it easy either. Some would get behind our cars and spin us out, others would point their taser out the window and fry the car with everyone in it," he re-lived the scene with horror in his eyes. "Once they were taking us back to the prison,

I heard the guards whispering about executing us to make an example of what happens to people that escape! Right before they got us back in the prison gates, I managed to slip away from the group, somehow not getting caught, and I found my way here," Luke finished.

"Honestly Luke," Cole started, while rubbing his sleepy eyes, "it sounds like they let you escape so they can bait us back."

"But how do we know that they aren't going to kill them?" Nub panicked.

"Look, either way, we are going to have to get them out," Cole responded calmly, already thinking up a plan.

"I don't know how long we have though. We know how crazy that Bacon Head is," Luke said with worry.

Nub nodded his head in agreement.

"So how are we going to make it there?" Nub asked. "Only one out of the three police cars has enough fuel in it, and the only helicopter that made it back got ruined during the landing," Nub said, staring at Cole.

Suddenly Luke's head shot up.

"You know, I think I might have the perfect solution to that," He said with a smirk.

Chapter 8

"Here we are, boys," Luke said gesturing to what was in front of them.

Cole, Nub, and a few of the other escapees followed Luke about 15 minutes away from their safe house, deep into the blistering hot desert.

With their jaws dropped, both Nub and Cole stared at a stash of dirt bikes and dune buggies, just sitting there waiting for them.

"Where'd these come from?" Cole asked, picking his jaw up from the ground.

"I don't care," Nub said, practically drooling. "I call driving."

"Um, no!" Cole responded harshly.

"Why not?" Nub asked, offended.

"Because I'm driving," he answered with a smirk.

"Boys, everybody can drive, there's enough of them for everyone," Luke laughed. "Now who's ready to re-save our friends!"

Chapter 9

"Here he comes," Cole said, looking into the distance towards the police car that was arriving at the prison gates.

Nub, Cole, and seven other escapees were propped up on a hilltop, sitting in their individual dune buggy, or dirt bike. Below them, they watched Luke, who was disguised as a police officer, pull into the main gate of the prison.

Luke parked his police car, jumped out the door, and sprinted back to the gate control room, which was between the entrance and exit gate. He opened the door and ran in fists flying.

"Never thought I'd be trying to break back into prison," Cole said shaking his head.

Right then the gate house door reopened, and a big thumbs up came out of it.

"Well friends," Nub started with a deep breath, "let's do this thing," he chuckled.

The surrounding area got filled with the sound of engines igniting, which for someone in the prison, would sound like a thousand giant hornets swarming right for you.

◆ "Let's roll out!" Nub shouted above the noise and signaled with his hands.

All eight vehicles peaked over the hill and started gaining speed toward a natural dirt ramp.

"HERE WE GO!" Cole shouted out of his dune buggy.

He launched off the ramp and sailed over the tall prison gates. One by one each person landed on top of the bright orange prison roof and kept driving.

After dodging a few chimney spouts, Cole took a right turn and jumped off the roof, into the courtyard. His buggy landed close to home plate, and he, with the other vehicles in tow, did a perfect drift around the whole kickball field. Cole lined his vehicle up with the locked courtyard doors that led inside, then he floored the accelerator and braced for impact!

"YEEEE HAW!" Cole screamed as his buggy crashed through the doors and came to a halting stop before slamming into the cement wall. All the other escapees parked their vehicles nicely, and rushed through the toppled doors, back into the prison!

"Knock them out, and take their key card and taser!" Nub ordered as he delivered a complimentary uppercut to a panicked guard.

The group made quick work of the guards in that area, then started making their way over to the cell block.

"Any minute now the alarms will be going off, so be prepared just in case there is a guard hiding behind a corner," Nub warned, taser in hand.

Just when he said it, the oh too familiar high pitched scream of the prison alarms started blaring.

"We have a group of intruders heading toward the cellblock. Backup needed immediately," someone said on the intercom system.

The group started sprinting to the cell block in order to get there before the mass of guards did.

"Alright! Here we are!" Nub said while holding his key card over the door scanner.

When the doors opened, Nub expected to see all of the recaptured prisoners just sitting in their cells, waiting for the impending execution, but that wasn't the case.

All of the cells were empty. Where'd they go? Did the guards take them? Have they been executed already?

Nope. Standing inches from the door was the whole group of prisoners with Emma in the front and a key card in her hand.

"What are you doing out?" Nub asked, surprised.

"What do you mean 'What are you doing out'?" Emma asked back, with an offended look on her face.

"I mean, uh," Nub stumbled.

"We're escaping of course! What about y'all? What are you doing here?" she asked, while grinning.

"Well, we were going to help you all escape," Nub answered, still surprised.

"Well you're doing a great job," she laughed, while waving her hands around, signaling the alarms.

"We're just going loud and proud," Cole winked.

"Alright, enough talking, we gotta get outa' here," the big prisoner named Tinsel said.

"Yeah, let's go," Nub agreed.

They handed the now ex-prisoners some of the extra tasers they collected from the downed guards and started jogging back to the crashed courtyard doors.

"Watch out!" Cole warned.

Just in front of them, a doo
up and a big stream of guara
flooding in.

"Find some cover!" Nub ordered as
he ran to a toppled table.

Nub aimed down his taser's sights,
pulled the trigger, and sent a nice jolt
of electricity into one of the guards.

It turned into a full-on firefight. Taser
barbs were flying in every direction,
and people from both sides were on
the ground as they got electrocuted.

The tide started to go in the prisoner's
favor as they started to work as a
team. If one of them got hit, their
teammates would yank the taser barbs
out before it could fry them too bad!

"Duck!" Emma screamed at Cole.

A pair of taser barbs went whizzing
over his head.

"Thanks!" he shouted back, trying to be heard over what sounded like a hundred pocket-sized lightning storms.

Before long all of the guards were on the ground, either surrendered or unconscious, and the group of escapees continued their journey back to the courtyard.

"Almost there!" Cole guided as they walked further down another hallway.

They had one more turn to take and then they were there. The whole group was practically in a sprint now. They turned, expecting a fast getaway, but instead, there was a whole wall of advanced, taser-proof riot shield wielding SWAT guards that were blocking them from their exit point.

Cole and a few others fired some shots, but the barbs just bounced off the shields.

Nub started to wonder if the whole plan had failed, but then a deep voice rang out.

"FOR FREEDOM!"

Cole looked over and saw Tinsel charging straight into the wall of shields.

"'MURICA!" Cole shouted as he too started sprinting towards the wall.

Then the whole group of escapees joined in. Tinsel bashed down 5 guards in the first push and started swatting down others as if they were flies.

Cole jumped onto one guy and started wrestling him down to the ground, and since there was an opening in the shield wall, the other prisoners started tasing them in the open spots.

Between Tinsel's sheer power, and the effective strength of the tasers, all the guards were taken care of in a matter of seconds.

"Let's get going!" Emma said with a grin. One by one the group exited the building and went towards their vehicles. Nub was the last in line. Right before he went through the opening, something familiar caught his eye. Standing at the back of the hallway, taser in hand, stood his nemesis: Bacon Head.

"Hey buddy," Nub said as he turned away from the exit and slowly started walking towards Bacon Head.

No answer.

"You don't say much do you?" Nub probed.

They got within 15 feet of each other and Nub stopped.

They both were armed with their tasers, but they kept their hands at their waists.

The Cowboy, Mexican standoff music started playing and Nub was pretty sure he saw a tumbleweed skirting across the concrete floor.

"Let's both draw at the same time," Nub said, hoping Bacon Head understood.

"Three," he took a quick breath.

"Two," he widened his stance.

"One-"

ZAAAP
ZAP
ZAP
ZAAAP

Bacon Head collapsed to the ground. He had taser barbs sticking out of his bum cheeks, and behind him was Cole having the time of his life.

"WHAT WAS THAT FOR?" Nub shouted at Cole.

"I'm sorry," Cole apologized while still laughing. "I was just going to get myself a helicopter, but then I saw him standing there and I couldn't resist," He said, wiping his eyes from laughing so hard.

"You took my revenge from me," Nub whined, while also chuckling.

"Well, you could tase him again," Cole offered.

"Nah, I might as well spare him," Nub said generously. "Let's just hope we don't see him around anytime soon."

"For real though," Cole chuckled. "I'll catch you back at the safe house," he said, before going off to steal himself a fresh helicopter.

Nub hopped inside his dune buggy, with Emma in the passenger seat, and drove out through the courtyard gate that Luke opened from the control room. The crew picked up Luke, and sped out of the prison gates, hopefully for the last time.

Chapter 10

They made it back to the safe house and started treating wounds and settling down.

Even though all the windows and doors were closed, a cold breeze started circulating around the room.

"Who turned the AC on?" Nub asked as he started getting chilly.

"I don't think that's air conditioning," Cole said slowly, as he looked around the room.

A bluish fog started emerging from walls and began lazily circulating around the room.

"What's happening?" Emma asked, standing up from her bed.

"Well, from what I've heard, this is what happens when we finish whatever the Server Nexus wants us to," Cole answered, starting to get excited. "Apparently we are going to be sucked back into the Nexus until it takes us to another world!"

The blue fog was getting thicker and thicker to where Nub couldn't see his feet anymore.

"Well, will we ever be able to see each other again?" Nub asked.

"I guess we can only hope so," Cole said with a smile. "If there's one thing I know, it's that we make a pretty good team!"

"I agree, it's been a blast meeting and working with you all," Nub nodded.

"Same here!" Emma piped in.

By now the fog was past their chest, and everything was getting pixelated.

"Until next time friends!" Nub shouted above the sound of rushing wind.

"Bye!" Emma waved.

"Peace!" Cole shouted back.

Then they all got sucked back into the server nexus, until the next adventure!

Acknowledgments

Shoutout to my family for encouraging
me to write a book.

Mr. Jesse for his awesome editing.

The creators of Jailbreak for making
such a dope game.

And of course the Nub Squad for all of
your support! Without you, none of this
would have happened. It has truly been a
life changing experience for me, and I
love putting a smile on every one of your
faces with each video I post!

Made in the USA
Middletown, DE
05 August 2020